Jeff Tracy was an engineer and [...] something to help people in n[...] a vast fortune in business, he spent billions secretly constructing a fleet of five Thunderbirds – amazing machines invented by his friend Brains, the world's top scientific genius. Thus International Rescue came into being. From its base on a luxurious Pacific island, this secret organization is always ready to speed to the aid of anyone in peril.

Each craft is unique. Thunderbird One, piloted by Scott Tracy, can race to the scene of a disaster at nine times the speed of sound. Often it is followed by Thunderbird Two, manned by Virgil Tracy, which brings an array of special rescue machines aboard its equipment pod. When catastrophe looms in space, Alan Tracy rockets to the rescue in Thunderbird Three. And for undersea calamities, there is the versatile one-man submarine Thunderbird Four, operated by Gordon Tracy. Last but not least, Thunderbird Five, orbiting far up in space, is manned by John Tracy, constantly on the alert to pick up distress signals from their agent in England, Lady Penelope. Together with her butler, Parker, she maintains the strict secrecy that is essential for the successful operation of International Rescue.

No matter what the risk to themselves, and in spite of the opposition of master criminals like The Hood, Jeff and his sons have pledged to give their aid to anyone in danger. And so, when earthquakes, fires, crashes or explosions threaten human life, the signal goes out: 'Calling International Rescue…' and then THUNDERBIRDS ARE GO!

THUNDERBIRDS™

ATLANTIC INFERNO 4

THIS IS A CARLTON BOOK

This edition published by Carlton Books Limited 2001
20 Mortimer Street
London
W1T 3JW

Reprinted in 2001.

First published in the UK by Transworld Publishers 1992
This edition of Thunderbirds: Atlantic Inferno is published by arrangement with
Transworld Publishers, 61–63 Uxbridge Road, London W5 5SA.

Design copyright © 2001 Carlton Books Limited
Text copyright © 2001 Dave Morris

™ and © 1965 and 1999. THUNDERBIRDS is a trademark of Carlton International
Media Limited and is used under licence.
THUNDERBIRDS is a Gerry Anderson Production.
Licensed by Carlton International Media Limited.
©1999. The Carlton logotype device is a trademark of Carlton International Media
Limited.

A CIP catalogue for this book is available from the British Library.

ISBN 1 84222 222 8

Editorial: Terry Burrows
Design: Adam Wright
Production: Janette Davis

THUNDERBIRDS™

ATLANTIC INFERNO 4

Dave Morris

CHAPTER ONE
ATLANTIC INFERNO

Jeff,' said Lady Penelope over the video-phone one day, 'when was the last time you took a holiday?'

Jeff had to think about that. Generally he wasn't much of a one for holidays. There was always too much work to be done – going over designs for new machines with Brains, refining International Rescue's procedures, organizing missions... Jeff could think of one time he'd been away from Tracy Island recently, on a trip to look at a new monotrain, but that was really business rather than pleasure.

'Admit it,' said Penelope. 'You can't remember, can you?'

Jeff shrugged. 'It's not that simple, Penny. A disaster might happen anywhere in the world at any time. I'm needed here to organize things if that happens.'

The viewscreen showed Penelope in the back of FAB1, her plush pink limousine. Behind her, a striking landscape was streaking past. 'Where are you, anyway?' Jeff went on, trying to change the subject.

'I'm in Australia, Jeff,' replied Penelope, 'and your rather obvious attempt to get off the hook is not going to work. That's exactly why I'm calling. You see, I'm on my way to spend a couple of weeks on my ranch here. I think it would be an excellent idea if you were to come too.'

'But, Penny,' said Jeff, shaking his head doggedly, 'I've just explained why that isn't possible.'

Scott, sitting reading nearby, had overheard the whole conversation. 'Oh, come on, Dad,' he called over his shoulder. 'We'd all still be here, and we all know the procedures. International Rescue can get by without you for a fortnight.'

Virgil was standing by the window, working on a painting of the sunlit Pacific scenery outside. Now it was his turn to chip in: 'I agree with Scott, Father. You're always working too hard. A rest would do you good.'

'What is this – a conspiracy?' snapped Jeff. 'Even my own sons are trying to get rid of me!'

'The boys agree with me, Jeff,' said Penny over

the video link. Her voice had taken on that no-nonsense tone which fitted perfectly with her aristocratic English accent. 'Now, let's have no more arguments. I shall expect you at my Australian ranch this evening. I *insist.*'

Jeff opened his mouth to answer, but before he could say anything, the screen went blank. 'How do you like that?' he blustered to his sons. 'She hung up on me!'

Scott tossed down his book and came over to Jeff's desk. 'Well, what do you expect, Dad?' he said. 'She was only thinking of you. You got her pretty annoyed by refusing like that.'

Jeff spread his hands helplessly. He could handle the most complicated of emergencies, but Lady Penelope was still capable of taking him by surprise. And he had rarely taken a break in twenty years. What with raising his family and setting up International Rescue, there had never been the time. Virgil seemed to know exactly what his father was thinking. 'We're all adults now, Father,' he said, 'and we can be trusted to run things if you take a holiday. It's precisely because you've done such an excellent job in organizing International Rescue that you can rely on it to run smoothly while you're away.'

'Sure!' said Scott, seeing that Virgil's words were getting through. 'And, Dad, you work so hard that you're wearing yourself out. The whole show will be that much the better for your taking a break. You'll get back from Australia refreshed and ready to take on twice as much work, if you have to.'

At that moment, Alan and Tin-Tin came in from the tennis court. Alan had caught the tail-end of the conversation. 'Did someone mention holidays?' he said, swishing his racquet in the air. 'Couldn't do without them. You know what they say about all work and no play…'

Jeff gave a big sigh. 'All right, all right! I'll go

to Penny's ranch. Scott, you'll be in charge while I'm away. Alan will pilot Thunderbird One if it's needed. Oh, and if they need me…'

'Dad, will you relax?' said Scott. 'I'm sure I and the boys will be able to cope with anything that comes up.'

After they had all watched Jeff's Learjet streak off into the southern sky, Scott went to sit behind his father's desk. It was a strange feeling, being completely in charge of International Rescue. Scott had been trusted with a huge responsibility, and he was determined not to let his father down. If only his stomach didn't feel like there was a bunch of butterflies skittering around inside it. Alan, at least, had confidence in his older brother. 'Well, Scott,' he said. 'What are you going to do first?'

Scott thought for a moment. What would his father do? Then he knew: 'I ought to call up

John in Thunderbird Five and see if anything's happening that we should know about.'

Scott flicked a switch that would open the communication link to Thunderbird Five. The portrait of John Tracy on the wall changed to a moving TV image.

'Hi, Scott,' said John.

'Hi, John. I thought I ought to let you know Dad's gone off on holiday. I'm in charge of things while he's away.'

'On holiday?' repeated John, cocking his eyebrows in amazement. 'I didn't think he knew the meaning of the word. Still, what can I do for you?'

'Oh, it's just a routine call. I wondered if there were any emergencies coming up…' Scott let his voice trail off. Even as he said it, he realized how foolish the question was. If there had been any problems, John would have already let him know. Maybe this leadership thing was going to

be harder than he thought.

'I'm not in the fortune-telling business yet, Scott,' John said with a chuckle. 'There's no news at all, really. The World Navy is getting ready for some manoeuvres in the South Atlantic, but I doubt if that's anything that need concern us.'

The World Navy hadn't had a serious accident

in twenty years. Scott knew that his brother only mentioned the Atlantic manoeuvres to restore Scott's self-assurance, since it was obvious to everyone that the call to Thunderbird Five was unnecessary. 'Thanks, John,' he said hastily, already reaching to shut down the communication link. 'Keep us posted if anything comes up.'

In the Atlantic Ocean, the World Navy fleet was getting into position for manoeuvres. Both ships and submarines were to be put through their paces in a series of gruelling tests. They were trying out new radar equipment, computers and weaponry in as close a simulation of real-life battle conditions as could be managed. The fact that there hadn't been a serious conflict in almost two decades did not mean that the Navy could relax. After all, their motto was 'Always Vigilant'.

On the bridge of his flagship, the *Illustrious*, Admiral Cook raised his binoculars and scanned the horizon. In the distance – perhaps twenty kilometres away – he could make out the distinctive shape of a drilling rig. 'Get on to the superintendent of that rig,' he ordered the radio operator. 'Tell him we're about to conduct an underwater test firing some nuclear torpedoes. There might be a slight tremor on the sea bed, but assure him that it's nothing for him to worry about.'

The admiral had had to contend with irate rig superintendents before. With the pockets of natural gas discovered under the ocean floor, new drilling rigs were being built every year. It was getting so that you could hardly find room in the sea to sail a fleet. And every time a missile was fired or a torpedo exploded, all the rig superintendents in that part of the sea would immediately get on their radios and start complaining. Privately, Admiral Cook had no time for them, but he'd learned that it was better to give them a friendly warning than to have to listen to their griping later.

More than a hundred fathoms deep, the nuclear submarine *Meteor* was moving into position for the test. As its radar picked up the approach of a remote-controlled target vessel, the *Meteor*'s captain gave an order and two sleek torpedoes detached themselves from the prow. They continued gliding alongside the *Meteor* like two pilot fish accompanying a shark.

'Target vessel in range,' reported the *Meteor*'s first officer.

'Fire torpedoes,' the captain replied.

The two torpedoes shot away like bloodhounds that had been let off their leash. However, even as they closed on their target vessel, the first officer could see from his instruments that one of them was wavering off course.

'Detonate it by remote,' said the submarine captain when he heard this.

It was the standard safety procedure to make sure a torpedo did not go wild and hit something else. But just as the first officer pressed the abort button, the other torpedo struck the target vessel, creating a small nuclear explosion. A sudden pulse of radio waves from the explosion scrambled the abort signal. The second torpedo streaked past the wreckage of the target.

'It's gone rogue! The torpedo's out of control!' was the message relayed to Admiral Cook abroad his flagship.

There was no time to do anything – there was nothing anybody *could* do. The torpedo collided with a rock outcropping on the sea bed and released the full force of its kiloton warhead. Cracks appeared in the ocean floor, and from the bridge of the *Illustrious* it was as though a lightning flash had crackled deep down beneath the sea. The shockwave reached them only moments later, and even the mighty flagship swayed with the impact.

Minutes later, the same shockwave reached the drilling rig *Seascape*. Frank Hooper, the rig superintendent, was furious. He had half expected the Navy to mess up one of their 'darn fool tests', as he called them. In his opinion they were like children playing with dangerous toys. Now one of those toys had gouged a chunk out of the sea bed and sent twenty-foot waves dashing against the supports of the rig.

Hooper started yelling orders. Sirens sounded an amber alert, warning the entire crew of the *Seascape* to man their stations. Storm anchors were fired, securing the rig against the buffeting waves, and the telescopic supports were raised by twenty feet to keep the structure from flooding. As he watched the sun set, Hooper felt more and more annoyed. He and his men would not get

much rest tonight, thanks to the World Navy's bungling.

Later, the swell on the ocean died down, and the panic died with it. Hooper was still fuming over the Navy's carelessness, but felt secure enough to stand the rig down from amber alert. The control room was quiet. The radio operator had nothing to report, and the seismograph showed the tremors in the sea bed had settled. Hooper stood by the window, peering out into the night.

Suddenly, without warning, the sky lit up like day as an enormous firejet shot straight up from the sea.

'Oh no!' gasped Hooper. 'That explosion must've weakened the sea bed after all. It looks like the gas field has blown!'

CHAPTER TWO
JUDGEMENT CALL

Jeff Tracy had arrived at Lady Penelope's ranch at dusk. Tired after his flight, he had been grateful for a light supper and then the chance to doze in front of the television for a few hours. Lady Penelope was content to leave conversation until the next day. She knew that Jeff needed a good rest more than anything.

With the TV tuned to a music programme, she sat flipping through a stack of magazines while Jeff lounged on the sofa.

An announcer appeared on the TV screen. 'We interrupt this programme to bring you a news flash,' he said. 'Reports are coming in that a gas field in the Atlantic has leaked, and a firejet over two hundred feet high is threatening drilling rigs in the area. The cause of the firejet is not yet certain, but it may be connected with an atomic explosion during World Navy manoeuvres.'

'Shall I wake Mr Tracy, milady?' said Parker to Lady Penelope as the music programme resumed.

'Don't you dare, Parker!' Penelope retorted. 'He's come here for a holiday, to get away from that sort of thing.'

They were both surprised when Jeff spoke without opening his eyes: 'It's OK, Parker,

I heard the whole newsflash anyway.'

'Jeff,' said Penelope, 'I thought you were asleep.'

Jeff sat up and stretched. 'Oh, years of one emergency after another have taught me to wake up instantly if there's any kind of trouble. But you can relax, Penny – I'm not worried about that firejet. Nobody has been hurt, and Scott can be relied on to keep an eye on the situation. He'll realize that this is *not* a job for International Rescue.'

On Tracy Island, Scott had received the news of the firejet from Thunderbird Five. After consulting with Brains, Scott tried to decide what his father would do in the same situation. Of course, Scott could have just phoned Jeff in Australia, but he had gone to Lady Penelope's ranch to get a rest from such problems. Also, Scott wanted to prove he could make the right decision without his father's help.

'Go and get the others,' he told Brains at last. 'I reckon this is a job for International Rescue.'

Soon Alan, Virgil and Gordon were dressed and standing by the desk listening to Scott's briefing. Alan in particular was raring to go. He was keen to try out Thunderbird One on a real mission, since he had previously only flown it for a few test runs. 'I can be there by dawn,' he told Scott.

Scott nodded. 'OK, Alan, you might as well set out right away,' he said. 'Virgil, you and Gordon take Pod Four and the sealing device, and follow Thunderbird One. Alan can fill you in on the details by radio once he's got a first-hand look at the situation. In the meantime, I'll get in touch with the rig superintendent and find out what's happening on the *Seascape*.'

Alan strode over to a special section of wall and turned to stand with his back to it, at the

same time reaching up to grasp a pair of
wall-lamps. There was a soft click as he tugged at
the lamps, and then the wall section revolved,
turning Alan around into a large bay.
Thunderbird One stood ahead of him. Alan felt
a tingle of excitement as the gantry extended
automatically, taking him directly into the cockpit
of the craft.

As the gantry retracted, Thunderbird One was already sliding diagonally down on a conveyor belt which took it into its underground launch bay. Alan tilted back in his chair. Above he could see a crack of silver pre-dawn sky, widening by the second as the swimming pool concealing the entrance to the launch bay was winched aside.

Alan keyed in the ignition sequence. The whole craft trembled into life as its mighty thrusters began to fire up.

'Thunderbird One, you are clear for take-off,' said Scott's voice over the radio.

Alan reached out for the controls. He had expected to feel nervous, since the slightest slip during launch could send Thunderbird One slamming into the side of the exit shaft at hundreds of miles an hour. In fact he felt nothing but the excitement of being in charge of the foremost of the Thunderbirds.

He pulled back the controls. The rockets spat

fire into the blast-proof pad beneath him. Thunderbird One reared up. Alan saw the edge of the swimming pool slide by, then – faster now, as he picked up speed – he glimpsed the house and the peak of the island. Then he was shooting up and up into a sky now tinged with the first golden streaks of sunlight.

He turned the nose of Thunderbird One into the west. Although nearly dawn here, it would still be dark out in the Atlantic. Alan was racing the sunrise to the scene of the disaster. He almost laughed out loud from the sheer thrill of it. *Maybe*, he thought, *Dad'll enjoy his holiday so much that he retires and puts Scott in charge all the time. Then I'd get to be the pilot of this baby. Wow – what a thought!*

Alan caught sight of the firejet several minutes before he arrived at the scene. It was quite a sight – breathtaking to look at, a flickering geyser flame stretching up as high as an office block. It would have been beautiful had it not been for the danger it presented.

Alan got clearance to land Thunderbird One on the *Seascape*'s helicopter pad and it was only a matter of minutes before he was setting up a mobile communications unit in the rig's control room.

'What's the next step?' asked Hooper.

'We wait for my brothers to arrive,' Alan told him. He picked up the radio mike and spoke into it: 'International Rescue base from *Seascape*. There's just one firejet as reported, Scott. The sealing device should handle it.'

'Great!' replied Scott over the radio. 'How soon is Virgil set to arrive?'

'I can hear Thunderbird Two's jets now,' Alan reported. 'Shall I give him the go-ahead to proceed as planned?'

'Sure thing. Good luck, you guys.'

Gordon was already aboard Thunderbird

Four inside its pod. As Virgil received the go-ahead, he cruised low over the ocean and threw the switch that released Pod Four. It fell with a soft splash, before the door dropped open allowing Thunderbird Four to slide down into the water.

For this operation, a new machine developed by Brains had been tethered to the back of Thunderbird Four by strong cables. It looked like nothing so much as a giant plug. And in a sense that's exactly what it was.

Gordon submerged and set a course towards the firejet. Dials on his control panel told him the sea was getting hotter as he approached it, but it was nothing the underwater Thunderbird could not handle.

Gordon noticed the seaweed in this part of the sea was withered by the heat. Then he saw the base of the firejet ahead of him – a spout of blue flame emerging from a hole in the sea bed. As they had guessed, the hole looked just like the kind of impact crater that would have been caused by a nuclear torpedo.

'It's weird!' said Gordon over the radio. 'Imagine a flame so hot that it burns even under the sea…'

'How about that sealing device?' Scott replied. 'Can you manoeuvre it over the hole?'

Gordon saw straight away that he would not be able to steer his craft right through the flame. On the other hand, he did not necessarily have to tow the sealing device directly behind him. By heading in the direction of the firejet and then angling away at the last moment, he could rely on the sealing device's momentum to carry it into position over the hole.

It was a simple operation for a skilled submariner like Gordon. 'It's in place,' he announced over the radio. 'I'm jettisoning the cables. Preparing to fire the rocket clamps now.'

The sealing device was resting on the hole. Burning gas was still escaping through a valve set into the sealing device, but the firejet was much smaller now. Cables connecting the sealing device to Thunderbird Four dropped away like fronds of seaweed. Then, in response to a remote control command, four rocket-powered piledrivers sank deep into the ocean floor at each corner of the device. It was now pinned securely in place over the hole.

'Close the valve completely, Gordon,' said Scott.

Gordon turned another remote control. The valve in the centre of the sealing device constricted, then closed altogether. The flame was choked off.

The result, as viewed from the *Seascape*, was spectacular. It seemed as though the raging firejet had just been snuffed out like a candle.

'You did it!' said Hooper to Lana. 'What was

that device of yours?'

Alan grinned. 'I guess you could say it's kind of like a big metal sticking plaster on the ocean floor. Or like sewing a patch on a torn jacket. And it's built to last. You won't have to worry about that firejet again.'

'That's a relief,' said Hooper. 'I've got to hand it to you International Rescue fellows – you sure know your stuff.'

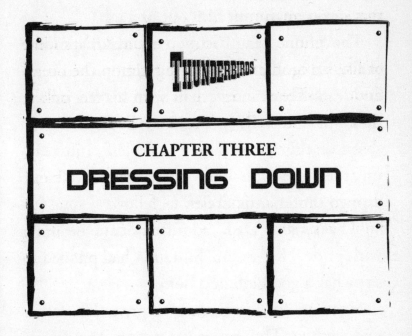

CHAPTER THREE

DRESSING DOWN

Once the whole team were assembled back on Tracy Island, everyone was falling over themselves to congratulate Scott.

'You did a great job!' Virgil told him.

'That's right, Scott,' Alan agreed. 'You directed the whole operation perfectly and you didn't put a foot wrong. I guess Dad had better watch out – you might put him out of a job.'

The phone rang. Scott, still basking in the praise his brothers were giving him, picked it up and leaned back in his chair with his feet on the desk. 'Hi, Scott Tracy speaking,' he said.

'Scott, this is your father', said Jeff. 'I just saw on the television that International Rescue capped the Atlantic firejet.'

'That's right, Dad,' admitted Scott, beaming with pride. He was sure his father had phoned to say what a good job he'd done.

Scott was in for a nasty surprise. His father said sternly: 'That was quite wrong. You should never have got involved.'

'But listen, Dad…' protested Scott.

'No, you listen, son. International Rescue is not just a lot of clever machinery for putting out fires.'

'But that fire could have caused a disaster, Dad,' said Scott.

'We're not dealing with "could haves", Scott,' insisted his father. 'What International Rescue does is too important to risk the whole team being out on a fool's errand while a real disaster might *actually* be happening somewhere else in the world.'

'I'll try to think a bit more carefully next time,' Scott promised.

'There won't be a next time. I'm cutting short my holiday and flying back immediately.' And with that, Jeff hung up.

Scott put the phone down and shook his head, bewildered. He'd been so sure he had made the right decision. Now he felt bad – not least because it looked as though his mistake had spoiled his father's holiday.

The Tracy brothers all looked at one another. 'Well, how do you like that?' said Gordon. 'Dad sounded pretty disgruntled.'

'Obviously he doesn't agree with Scott's

handling of the situation,' said Virgil. 'But for my money, Scott, I think you made the right decision sending us out there.'

Scott just sat there looking crestfallen. 'I wish I could be so sure, now,' he said.

A few minutes went by, and then the phone rang again. This time it was Lady Penelope. 'Scott, I've spoken to your father,' she began.

'Uh-huh, Lady Penelope.' Scott replied. 'I suppose he's already on his way back here.'

'No, I've managed to convince him that it would be a bad idea,' said Lady Penelope. 'He's just worried about International Rescue, Scott – it's his baby. But after giving you that dressing-down, I think he felt he'd been a trifle harsh. He knows he can trust you not to send the Thunderbirds out on a false alarm again.'

'OK, thanks, Lady Penelope,' said Scott, brightening at the news. 'Bye.'

'Well,' said Virgil, who had overheard the

conversation, 'it seems you're back in control, Scott.'

'Yes,' said Scott, 'And I've learned my lesson. Next time I'll make absolutely certain that International Rescue are really needed before committing us to a mission.'

Back on the *Seascape* drilling rig, Frank Hooper was one man who had no doubts about Scott's decision. 'That International Rescue – what an outfit!' he enthused. 'They probably saved our lives.'

'They certainly stoppered that firejet,' said Dick O'Shea, his second-in-command.

A third man, Jerry Kravitz, was not so sure. His face creased into a worried frown as he stared at the instruments on his control panel. 'Maybe you ought to take a look at this seismograph reading, Frank,' he called over.

Hooper glanced over at the screen. The

seismograph showed any movements in the Earth's crust. It was useful for detecting the location of gas pockets and also gave advance warning of earthquakes. There weren't supposed to be earthquakes in this part of the Atlantic, but the readings were going off the scale.

'There are multiple tremors running right across the extent of the gas field,' said Hooper.

O'Shea nodded. 'If this keeps up, it'll open another crack in the sea bed!'

The words had hardly left his mouth when the sky lit up with a roaring blue flame. Everyone aboard the rig stared at it, aghast. It was clearly much nearer than the first firejet had been. And bigger. They could feel the wave of heat coming off it.

Hooper turned to the radio operator with a look of horror on his face. 'Call International Rescue,' he said. 'And hurry… or it may be too late.'

Scott was astonished when the call was relayed to him from Thunderbird Five. 'How could it happen, Brains?' he said. 'Surely the sealing device couldn't fail?'

'It didn't fail, Scott,' said Brains, who was trying to puzzle out exactly what had happened even as he spoke. 'My guess is, er, the torpedo detonation caused unstable layers of rock in the sea bed to subside… creating pockets of gas that are, um, continuing to be ignited by the heat from the first firejet…'

'But why hasn't the whole gas field ignited?' asked Alan.

Brains adjusted his thick glasses as he did a few calculations on a notepad. 'It's hard to be definite,' he said, 'but it looks as though the fire is, er, travelling under the rock until it finds the next, er, weak point. That could well be, ah, *Seascape*.'

'So what can we do about it?' Virgil wanted to know.

'Well,' Brains explained, 'Thunderbird Four will have to go down and fire, er, strategically placed missiles into the sea bed. That will, um, fracture the layers of rock and prevent the, er, spread of the fire.'

'Like cutting a firebreak in a forest,' said Gordon.

For a change, Scott was the only one who didn't seem keen to jump into action. 'Why can't the Navy do that?' he said.

'They haven't, um, got the right equipment,' answered Brains. His natural modesty stopped him from pointing out that International Rescue's equipment was the best in the world.

'So we need to seal off the gas field to save *Seascape* from disaster,' said Virgil impatiently. 'What are we sitting around talking for? Let's go!' He started over towards the full-length picture that formed the secret entrance to Thunderbird Two's hangar.

'Now hold on, Virgil!' said Scott suddenly. 'There's an alternative plan. We can let the Navy evacuate *Seascape* and leave the fire to burn itself out. That way there's no danger to anybody, and we don't waste our resources on a needless mission.'

'Boy!' exclaimed Gordon. 'You've sure

changed your tune!' Scott's attitude astounded him, since his eldest brother was usually the first to act in a crisis.

Scott gave a rueful half-smile. 'Well, getting chewed out by Dad over the last affair has made me less reckless. I've decided this is definitely *not* a case for International Rescue.'

Back at the *Seascape*, things were moving from bad to worse. The tremors recorded by the seismograph showed that more layers of rock were slipping. A channel of gas was forming under the sea bed.

'It's getting close,' said Kravitz after studying the instruments. 'Maybe we ought to call the Navy – ask them to airlift us off the rig.'

'I already have,' said Hooper grimly, 'but they've moved several hundred miles north since yesterday. They can't get anyone to us sooner than a couple of hours.'

'I'm not sure we have that long,' said O'Shea. He was looking out over the sea at another firejet which had just erupted out of the water, this time only a few miles from *Seascape*.

It took nearly a minute for the giant wave sent out from the exploding firejet to reach the rig. The wave swept into the support columns with devastating force. If it had hit the coast, it would have torn whole buildings from their foundations. If it had hit a ship, it would have capsized it. Despite the rig's massive size, it shuddered like a toy. Then there was the torturing sound of twisting metal, and the whole structure tilted over. Everyone staggered from one side of the control room to the other, clutching on to whatever they could.

The rig was now leaning over a steep angle. Hooper got to his feet. 'One of the support columns must have slipped its shackles,' he said. 'As if we didn't have enough to worry about!'

'We'd better take a diving sphere down to inspect the damage,' said O'Shea.

They hurried out on to the deck of the rig. Men were scuttling about, urgently securing equipment that was teetering over. A few miles out, the firejet was spluttering blue flame into an overcast grey sky. Further tremors continued to shake the rig alarmingly.

Hooper yelled orders to the winch operator and then he and O'Shea climbed into the diving sphere. It was a dangerous job, going down in the water at a time like this, but somebody had to do it. It was vital to learn the extent of the damage. The government would want to repair *Seascape* if it was still standing after the fire burned out.

The crane swung the sphere out over the edge of the rig. A moment later, waves washed up past the porthole. They sank down through the murk until they could see the buckled support column.

'It looks bad, Dick,' said Hooper, whistling between his teeth.

'Yeah,' agreed O'Shea. 'I can count at least – what? – six shackle bolts that have sheared off at the base.'

'Well, we'd better get some divers down here. They can shore up the support and then get to work on temporary repairs.' Hooper reached for the button to signal the winch operator that they were ready to come back up.

Another shockwave thundered against the side of the rig. Giving a groan of weakened metal, it tilted another few degrees. In the diving sphere, Hooper and O'Shea felt as if they were on the inside of a giant's rattle. They were thrown against the side of the sphere as – its cables slackened by the wave's impact – it went plunging down to the bottom of the sea.

'Frank, are you all right?' said O'Shea. 'Another firejet must have gone up.'

'Ouch,' said Hooper, rubbing his head where he'd hit it on the side of the sphere. He pushed at the button again and again but there was no response. 'The winch controls won't respond.'

'The cables must have got tangled up. We're trapped down here, Frank. We've only one hope of getting out before the rig explodes – and that's International Rescue.'

CHAPTER FOUR
A REAL EMERGENCY

'O K, guys,' said Scott when he heard the news. 'Thunderbirds are go!'

None of the team needed telling twice. They were on their way to the hangars almost before the words left Scott's lips.

'You've certainly altered your, er, opinion, Scott,' said Brains as they watched the

Thunderbirds take off. 'How come?'

Scott's jaw was set in an expression of firm resolve. This time he *knew* he was doing what his father would have done. He could feel it. 'The lives of Hooper and O'Shea are certainly at risk, for one thing,' he explained. 'Also, we know that the fire is spreading. The bore hole directly under the rig is an obvious weak point, and when the fire gets there the *Seascape* will go up with one almighty bang. I'm not sure the Navy can airlift everyone off in time.'

It was nearly two hours before Alan radioed to say he had arrived at the rig. Scott, poring over the maps of the gas field with Brains, flipped the switch and Alan's portrait on the wall turned into a TV image.

'I'm about to touch down on the *Seaview*,' Alan reported. 'Virgil and Gordon are expected here in fifteen minutes.'

'Tell them they're going to have to move fast,'

said Scott, gulping at a cup of coffee he had forgotten about and left to go cold.

'Y-yes, Alan,' joined in Brains. 'We estimate there's, er, not much time before the fire reaches the bore hole of the rig.'

Alan moved Thunderbird One in over the sagging structure of the rig. The helipad was suspended on hydraulic columns that had partly corrected for the tilt of the rig, so it was safe to land, even though the Thunderbird would be resting on a slight incline. As Alan descended, he could already see a group of World Navy jets in the distance. They were coming to evacuate the men from *Seascape*. That was good; International Rescue had enough to worry about just getting Hooper and O'Shea to the surface, without having to deal with a full-scale airlift as well.

Once he had his Thunderbird down, Alan took a mobile radio unit and hastily made his way through the throng of panicking rig workers to the *Seascape*'s control room. Only Kravitz was still there, gazing in a mixture of awe and fear at the multiple firejets now raging out at sea.

Alan finished setting up the mobile unit just as a deep drone of powerful jets announced Thunderbird Two's arrival. He snapped open a multi-channel radio link between Tracy Island and all the Thunderbird crafts.

'Gordon,' said Scott as the system came on-line, 'you know what you have to do?'

Gordon was already at the controls of Thunderbird Four, waiting for Virgil to drop off the pod. 'Yes, Scott.'

Gordon could feel the vibration through Thunderbird Four's hull as the pod's locking bolts retracted. A few seconds of weightlessness were followed by a soft impact as the pod splashed down. Gordon started up his Thunderbird as the pod door swung open,

sliding rapidly forward off the launch ramp into the ocean. He wasted no time in diving. Powerful arc lamps on Thunderbird Four's prow began to scan the sea bed...

'I can see them!' Gordon said suddenly. 'But the diving sphere's trapped under half a ton of girders and other debris.'

'What about the hatch?' Scott asked him.

There was a pause before Gordon replied: 'No, it looks too badly damaged to open.'

Scott thought quickly. 'OK, Gordon, you're going to have to move the whole diving sphere out of the danger area. First sever the winch cables with the laser cutter, then get to work clearing the debris.' He turned to his youngest brother's portrait: 'Alan, how many more men are there still on the rig?'

'The navy helijets are moving them off fast, Scott. There are eight still to go – plus myself and Kravitz.'

Scott consulted Brains. There was a film of sweat on his face as he spoke to Alan again: 'There might only be a few minutes left, Alan, if our calculations are… Alan! Alan!'

Alan's picture had gone out of focus for a moment. The TV image was now crackling with static. 'I felt the rig shift then…' said Alan.

Scott's brow was furrowed with intense concentration as he pondered every aspect of the emergency. 'OK, there's nothing more for you to do there. The Navy will get the last men off, but I'm worried about Thunderbird One.'

'That's right!' said Alan. 'If the rig slips any further she might slip off into the sea!'

Scott nodded. 'Pack up the mobile control and get Thunderbird One airborne. Gordon, how's it going?'

Even in the midst of danger, the whole team were impressed by Scott's quick-fire control of the situation. 'I've got through the cables, Scott,' reported Gordon. 'I'm now clearing the debris around the sphere.'

'Don't take too long,' said Scott. 'Virgil, anything to report?'

Thunderbird Two was hovering over the ocean near the beleaguered *Seascape*. As Virgil looked out of the window, he could see gas bubbling up beside the rig. It was obvious that the bore hole was weakening. 'The whole rig's shifting again!' he cried. 'Thunderbird One's slipping off the helipad!'

Alan had just at that moment climbed into Thunderbird One's cockpit. He dived at the throttle and threw it on. The vertical jets screamed into life, thrusting the Thunderbird clear of the rig barely a split-second before the helipad collapsed entirely.

'Alan, are you all right?' Scott barked into the radio.

The force of the emergency take-off had thrown Alan to the floor of the cockpit. He clambered into his chair looking shaken but unhurt. 'Sure, Scott,' he said. 'But you'd better check Gordon. I'm afraid the whole rig might blow at any moment.'

Down in Thunderbird Four, Gordon could hear falling debris ringing against the hull.

Worse still, he could see a flicker of flame around the drilling shaft directly under the centre of the rig. But, like all the Tracy brothers, he had been trained by his father to focus entirely on the job in hand. Thoughts of his own peril hardly bothered him at all.

'Gordon,' said Scott over the radio. 'There's no time left! Get clear!'

Gordon gritted his teeth. There was just one last heavy girder to shift... and he certainly had no intention of abandoning those men in the sphere, no matter what. He slowly extended Thunderbird Four's electromagnets and clamped them on to the side of the sphere. Bubbles of hot escaping gas were muddying the water all around him now, making it almost impossible to see. But he felt the jarring of the electromagnets as they locked home.

From the air, Virgil and Alan gasped in unison. Before their eyes, the *Seascape* folded as

though it were made of cardboard, breaking apart as it fell into the sea. Then the gas rushing up the bore hole ignited, and there was a titanic explosion. A blossom of flame burst high into the air, sending out a waft of furnace-like heat that Alan and Virgil could feel even through the hulls of their Thunderbirds.

Scott was concerned. 'Gordon!' he screamed into the radio.

'I'm… OK,' replied Gordon, inwardly reciting a prayer now he had time to think of his close call. 'I managed to get clear in the nick of time. I'm surfacing with Hooper and O'Shea now.'

From there on it was plain-sailing. Virgil picked up the diving sphere with grapples and took it to the flagship *Illustrious* before returning to retrieve Gordon in Pod Four. Then all the Thunderbirds headed back to base. The mission had been a resounding success. All the men were safely evacuated from the rig before it blew, and the only problem now was a number of fires that would burn themselves out in time. The Tracy brothers had good reason to be pleased with themselves.

Back at Tracy Island a couple of hours later, they were surprised to find their father waiting to greet them, along with Scott and Brains. Alan was the first to find his tongue. 'Dad!' he said. 'I thought you were on holiday.'

'I was,' said Jeff, 'but when I heard on the radio there was a real emergency in the Atlantic, I thought I'd better hurry back and take charge. Luckily there was no need – Scott handled the whole thing so well I wasn't needed. Maybe I should get back to my holiday now…'

Scott leapt up from behind the desk and held the chair out for his father. 'No, Dad, you'll probably get more rest back at work than you've been getting on holiday,' he said hastily.

Jeff grinned as he sat down. 'Aren't you keen to stay in charge of International Rescue for a while, then, son?'

'No way!' said Scott. 'In fact, after all the excitement I think *I* need a holiday!'